JF
Marsh, Carole.
The mystery in Las Vegas

The Mystery in
LAS VEGAS

by
Carole Marsh

30 Years Ago . . .

As a mother and an author, one of the fondest periods of my life was when I decided to write mystery books for children. At this time (1979) kids were pretty much glued to the TV, something parents and teachers complained about the same way they do about web surfing and video games today.

I decided to set each mystery in a real place—a place kids could go and visit for themselves after reading the book. And I also used real children as characters. Usually a couple of my own children served as characters, and I had no trouble recruiting kids from the book's location to also be characters.

Also, I wanted all the kids—boys and girls of all ages—to participate in solving the mystery. And, I wanted kids to learn something as they read. Something about the history of the location. And, I wanted the stories to be funny. That formula of real+scary+smart+fun served me well.

I love getting letters from teachers and parents who say they read the book with their class or child, then visited the historic site and saw all the places in the mystery for themselves. What's so great about that? What's great is that you and your children have an experience that bonds you together forever. Something you shared. Something you both cared about at the time. Something that crossed all age levels—a good story, a good scare, a good laugh!

30 years later,
Carole Marsh

Christina "Mystery Girl" Mimi Papa Grant

Hey, kids! As you see—here we are ready to embark on another of our exciting Carole Marsh Mystery adventures! You know, in "real life," I keep very close tabs on Christina, Grant, and their friends when we travel. However, in the mystery books, they always seem to slip away from Papa and me so they can try to solve the mystery on their own!

I hope you will go to www.carolemarshmysteries.com and apply to be a character in a future mystery book! Well, the *Mystery Girl* is all tuned up and ready for "take-off!"

Gotta go...Papa says so! Wonder what I've forgotten this time?

Happy "Armchair Travel" Reading,

Mimi

Christina Yother **Grant Yother** **Liam Machado** **Maya Scarbrough**

ABOUT THE CHARACTERS

Christina Yother, 10, from Peachtree City, Georgia

Grant Yother, 7, from Peachtree City, Georgia, Christina's brother

Liam Machado, 11, from Peachtree City, Georgia, as Chandu

Maya Scarbrough, 10, from Fayetteville, Georgia, as Asha

The many places featured in the book actually exist and are worth a visit! Perhaps you could read the book and follow the trail these kids went on during their mysterious adventure!

TITLES IN THE CAROLE MARSH MYSTERIES SERIES

Books and Teacher's Guides are available at booksellers, libraries, school supply stores, museums, and many other locations!

CONTENTS

1 TIGER TRICKS

As an eerie green glow began to illuminate the stage, Christina watched a ghostly white fog roll toward her. The soft music was growing louder. Christina could not only hear it, she could feel it rumbling in her chest.

Suddenly, ice-blue eyes pierced the mist like blazing sapphires, burning a path for two slinking tigers. Completely white except for their black stripes, they looked more phantom than feline. Christina's younger brother, Grant, yelped. "You pinched my arm!"

"Owww!"

"Sorry," Christina mumbled, "I thought it was the chair's arm!" She brushed her long brown hair over her shoulders and settled back into her seat.

Christina knew this was only a rehearsal for the Mysteries Hotel Magic Show, but she couldn't help gripping the arms of her front-row seat in the darkness. This was her first trip to Las Vegas and it was exciting!

The owner of the hotel, Mr. Jenkins, was a friend of Christina and Grant's grandfather, Papa. Mr. Jenkins invited them to see the magic show rehearsal the minute they arrived at the hotel. They hadn't even been to their rooms yet!

Christina jumped as a booming voice announced, "Rescued from the jungles of India, they've come to share their magic with you! Ladies and gentlemen, meet the world's most regal and rare twins—Soman and Shiba!"

"Those are the most beautiful creatures I've ever seen," Christina said.

Grant's jaw dropped open as he watched the stage through binoculars. "W-w-wow," he stuttered.

"My turn," declared Mimi, the children's grandmother, peeking through Grant's binoculars.   "Oh, my," she added, "they are just magnificent!"

"Look!" Grant whispered to Christina, as a girl and boy entered from each side of the stage to meet the tigers. "They're just kids!"

Spotlights focused on two large, mirrored, rotating globes that shot spears of pink light into the dark auditorium.   The boy and girl commanded Soman and Shiba to jump onto the globes.

"And now," the announcer continued, "the only one these royal tigers bow to—the Maharaja of Magic, Manendra!"

Out walked a man in a sparkling blue costume and jeweled turban. Soman and Shiba changed from calm tigers to hissing, swatting beasts as he approached.

Manendra thrust his hands into the air and the fog crept back across the stage. Christina noticed two silver rings floating from the ceiling toward each of the tigers.

"I don't see any wires!" Grant exclaimed. "Do you see wires, Christina?"

As the rings neared the tigers, the music grew louder and a puff of silver smoke shot out of the globes where the tigers sat. The music stopped suddenly and the rings hit the floor with a thud. The tigers were gone!

"How'd they do that?" Grant said, clapping.

"Magic," Mimi answered.

When the music started again, Christina saw something else descending from the ceiling. It was the tigers! They had reappeared and were being lowered to the stage on small circular platforms.

"Come and bow!" the magician commanded. The tigers left their platforms obediently and bowed to Manendra. He patted each on the head and motioned for them to leave the stage.

Christina noticed the tigers were once again very calm. She expected the boy and girl to escort the tigers away, but two men who were not in costumes led them offstage.

"Give me those binoculars!" Christina ordered, before Grant had time to take them off his neck.

"You're choking me!" Grant exclaimed.

"Oh! Sorry, Grant," Christina said.

It was hard to tell with the stage lighting, but as Christina took a closer look at the tigers, they looked different. She had the feeling something wasn't right!

2 TRACKING THE TEARS

"So, what did you think, kids?" Mr. Jenkins asked, as soon as the house lights came on.

"It was awesome!" was Grant's quick reply.

Despite her strange feeling that something was wrong, Christina agreed. "Mr. Jenkins, everyone will want to see Soman and Shiba!"

"I know you folks are tired and ready to get to bed," Mr. Jenkins observed. "Your luggage and room keys are at the check-in desk. I'll see you at breakfast tomorrow morning."

Walking from the hotel theater to the desk was a new experience for Grant and Christina. Following a red, tiled path, they moved into a huge room as dark and cool as a cave. On each side, coins clattered, bells clanged and lights flashed. The constant hum of people talking was occasionally interrupted by joyous screams.

"What is this place?" Grant asked, his blue eyes opened wide. "I've never seen so much bling-bling! And it's so loud in here!"

"This is the hotel casino," Mimi said. "Almost every hotel in Las Vegas has one." She slung her beaded red shawl over her shoulders. "I'm too tired to explain tonight. I'll tell you all about it later, OK?"

"Yep, little doggies," said Papa, looking tall and rugged in his black cowboy hat and chocolate-brown leather boots. "It's time to hit the sack!"

Christina knew how Mimi felt. She had felt like she was coming down with a cold since they left their home in Georgia. But Christina didn't want anyone to know she didn't feel well. She and Grant had worked too hard to be included on this trip.

Christina and Grant often traveled with Mimi and Papa. Mimi wrote mysteries for children, and often traveled to do research for her books. But this trip to visit Papa's old friend, Mr. Jenkins, and one of the country's largest air shows, Aviation Nation, at Nellis Air Force Base near Las Vegas, was a different story. Mimi had to be convinced it was a good idea!

Christina remembered the conversation almost word for word.

"Las Vegas is not a place for kids," Mimi had said.

"But, Mimi," Christina had replied, "it's not an adults-only town like it was when you were a kid. Now, there are roller coasters, chocolate factories, magic shows and lots of other things kids love. It's educational, too. We can even visit King Tut's tomb!"

Grant had also done his homework. "Did you know there are hotels in Las Vegas that look like New York, Paris and lots of other places?" he had piped in. "It's like every place in one place!"

Impressed by all the things the kids had learned, Mimi finally declared defeat. "You win!" she had told them. "Besides, a hotel called 'Mysteries' is the perfect place for a family of mystery solvers to visit," she added, referring to the kids' uncanny ability to get mixed up in a mystery wherever they traveled!

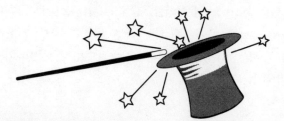

Grant and Christina dragged their luggage into the suite they were sharing with Mimi and Papa. Grant immediately started making footprints in the freshly vacuumed carpet.

"Do you think Clue could follow this trail?" he asked, thinking of their dog they had left at home.

Christina shuffled into the bathroom to brush her teeth. When she stopped to rinse, she heard a strange noise on the other side of the wall. The way it was echoing, she guessed it was coming from the stairwell next to their room.

"Did you hear that, Grant?" she asked her brother, who was now drawing tic-tac-toe shapes in the carpet.

"Hear what?" he asked, annoyed with the interruption.

"Come in here!" Christina said.

"It sounds like someone is crying," Grant observed. "I wonder what's wrong. Do you think someone fell down the stairs?"

"I didn't think of that!" Christina said. "We'd better go and see if they're OK." Christina grabbed their room card-key and they rushed to the stairwell.

Sad time in the stairwell!

A girl about Christina's age sat near the top of the stairs. Long ebony hair fell around her face like a black waterfall, almost touching the stairs as she rested her head on her knees. She wore a sparkling, ice-blue outfit.

"Are you all right?" Christina asked.

"Did you fall down the stairs?" Grant added.

"No, I didn't fall," the girl answered, lifting her head. Mournful brown eyes peered up at them. Her thick accent was a clue that she was probably not from Las Vegas.

"Did my crying wake you?" she asked.

"We weren't in bed yet," Christina answered. "We just got here."

"Why are you crying?" Grant asked, tired of chit-chat and wanting to get to the point.

"You're lucky," she said. "You just got here. I have to leave in a few short days. That's why I'm crying."

"Has your family been on vacation?" Christina asked.

"No," the sad girl answered. "My father works for a tiger rescue organization in India. We brought two rare, white tigers from India to star in this hotel's magic show. My father brought my brother and me along because we helped raise the tigers from cubs. They feel safe and calm with us around. That's why I am so sad to leave them here all alone in this strange country."

"You're the girl from the magic show!" Christina observed. "The tigers are amazing!"

"Why can't you just stay here?" Grant asked.

"My father has to get back to India, where he has other tigers to care for," the girl replied. "My mother is taking care of everything while my father's away. I am sad to leave the tigers, but I am ready to see my mother again."

The girl wiped the tears from her flushed cheeks. "There is a woman who will take my place when I go back to India," she added, "but Father said the tigers would be more comfortable with me at first. I have to wear this sparkly costume so they can get used to all the glitter."

The kids heard a door slam on the floor below and boots thumping up the stairs. Christina knew stairwells were not safe places late at night. Before she could herd Grant back to the room, a man appeared at the bottom of the stairs.

"Hello, Asha," he said. He too was dressed in a sparkling blue outfit. Christina recognized him as the magician from the show.

"I just tucked in your tigers," he said with a smile. "I think they're starting to like me." Christina noticed that Asha looked uncomfortable and did not return his smile.

"AH-CHOOO!!"

Before she knew it, Christina sneezed. As the man walked by, he reached in his pocket and handed her a tissue. "It's clean," he promised.

Asha stood up to leave. "Would you like to meet the tigers and my brother?" she asked.

"Are you kidding?" Christina replied, despite her stuffy nose. "You bet I would!"

Grant was just as excited. "Sure!" he said.

3 KIDNAPPED KITTIES

Christina and Grant followed Asha down a narrow alley. When they came to a locked gate, she pulled a key from around her neck and unlocked it.

"Whose house is that?" Grant asked, staring at what looked like a white palace.

"That's where Soman and Shiba live," Asha said. "Chandu, come and meet my new friends!"

There was no answer.

"Soman, Shiba, come!" Asha called out. Again, there was no response.

"That is strange," Asha said. "Soman and Shiba always come when I call."

Movement in the shadows caught Grant's eye. "Is that them over there?" he asked.

Asha walked to the other side of the enclosure and squinted through the chain-link fence. Two white tigers looked at her curiously, then hissed and growled.

"Look at his paw!" Asha exclaimed, pointing at the largest tiger's back foot. "I see orange! This is not Soman and Shiba! Someone has painted these imposters white!"

TAP! TAP

A muffled tapping sound drew Christina's attention. "Did you hear that?" she asked.

"I think it's coming from that direction," Grant said, running around the corner of a small storage building.

"I'll bet this is locked," Christina said, twisting the nearest door handle.

"This is Las Vegas," Grant replied. "Let's take a chance!"

To their surprise, the door opened! In the darkness, they could smell musty mops and cleaning supplies. They could also hear the noises they heard before, only louder.

"I can't see a thing!" Christina said. "Grant, open the door wider and let some light shine in."

With the light, Christina could see a shiny silver object on the other wall. It was another doorknob.

Startled by a loud noise, Christina and Asha turned to see Grant straddling a mop. "Grant to the rescue!" he cried, charging forward. He misjudged the distance and slammed into the door.

"Oh, Grant!" Christina said. "Let's hope our luck is still good," she added, as she twisted the knob. "Nope, out of luck." The door refused to open, but Christina's effort had caused the noises inside to grow louder.

"Can I help you?" a voice said from the open doorway. Grant, Christina and Asha jumped, but were relieved when they turned to see Mr. Jenkins.

"What are you kids doing here at this time of night?" Mr. Jenkins asked.

"Our tigers have been stolen!" Asha exclaimed.

"What?" Mr. Jenkins said in disbelief.

"Someone has taken Soman and Shiba!" Asha explained. "We had just discovered the imposters left in their place when we heard noises in here."

"Yes, I hear it too," Mr. Jenkins remarked. "I've got a key. Let's see what's going on in there."

When Mr. Jenkins opened the door, Christina saw a familiar sparkle in the faint light. As soon as Mr. Jenkins flipped the light switch, she knew what it was—the same sparkling blue cloth that made up Asha's costume was peeking between stacked cardboard barrels!

"Chandu, is that you?" Asha asked.

"Yes!" Chandu said, running around the barrels. "I was afraid you might be those men!"

Christina could see that Chandu looked a lot like his sister. She could also see the fear in his dark eyes.

Suddenly, they heard another muffled voice. "Don't forget me!"

"Our father is locked in that closet," Chandu said. As soon as Mr. Jenkins opened the door, the children gripped their father, Mr. Patel, in a bear hug.

"Who did this?" Christina asked.

"We were set for the end of the magic show," Chandu explained, "when a man told us we were needed here right away. When we got here, two men pushed us inside and locked the door."

"Did you see what they looked like?" Mr. Jenkins asked.

"We didn't see their faces," Mr. Patel answered. "It was too dark. But I think one of them was in a suit. I caught a glimpse of sequins on the other one's clothes and he had a very deep voice."

"That could describe almost anyone in Las Vegas," Mr. Jenkins remarked, whipping out his cell phone. "I'm calling the police."

4 KNEE-DEEP IN A MYSTERY

The next morning, it took Christina a few moments to realize she was in a hotel room. The night's events had left her exhausted. She swallowed hard to see if her throat was sore. It was.

Grant was still asleep and making his usual little-kid snoring noises.

She quietly got up and slipped on her favorite jeans that she had worn the night before, hoping that Mimi wouldn't notice. She fingered the sparkling rhinestones on her shirt that spelled, *"Viva Las Vegas!"* Before leaving their home in Georgia, Mimi had surprised the kids with matching shirts. Of course, they were in her favorite color, red.

Mimi had to translate the slogan for Grant. "It means, *Long Live Las Vegas*," she explained. "It's also the name of an Elvis Presley movie. Elvis spent a lot of time in Las Vegas." Christina knew Mimi was a fan of the King of Rock and Roll!

Papa had also given Grant a pair of cowboy boots and hat to match the ones he wore all the time. "A man in the West has to have his boots, jeans, and hat," he had said in his deep, booming voice.

Christina opened the door adjoining their room to their grandparents' room. Mimi and Papa were gone. But on the bed was a note:

See you
downstairs
for breakfast!

"It's about time you sleepy heads got up!" Papa said, as Christina and Grant shuffled into the dining room.

Grant rubbed his eyes in disbelief when he saw the breakfast buffet. Mountains of muffins, dozens of donuts and parades of pastries covered the table. Planks of bacon formed a bridge over a river of orange juice that flowed to a glimmering ice sculpture of a tiger. Watermelons carved like picnic baskets overflowed with strawberries, bananas, and every other kind of fruit imaginable.

"This must be breakfast heaven!" Grant exclaimed, stacking his plate with goodies. "Yum," Christina mumbled, as she bit into a blueberry

muffin as big as a softball. "Grant, you've got to try this." Grant couldn't resist the opportunity to make fun of his sister's new braces. "I'm glad you like it," he said, "because you've got enough stuff caught in those railroad tracks on your teeth to last through lunch and dinner!"

Christina whipped a tiny blue mirror out of her purse. "Oh, yuck," she murmured, frantically sliding her tongue across her braces to remove the muffin residue. "Braces!"

"I've just been telling your grandparents about the missing tigers," Mr. Jenkins said. "I had high hopes that our magic show would convince lots of families to stay here. Without the show, I may have to close this place. There are so many **elaborate** hotels and so much exciting entertainment in town, we've had a hard time drawing as many people as we need to survive."

"Well, there sure seems to be plenty of people in Las Vegas," Mimi said. "I can't believe how much this place has grown since my last visit."

"Yes," Mr. Jenkins said. "When Las Vegas became a town in 1911, only 1,500 people lived here. Can you imagine that?

"Now," he continued, "more than a million people call Las Vegas home and thousands of newcomers move here every month. And that doesn't even count the visitors who come for entertainment!"

"Since Las Vegas is in the desert, where does the water come from for all these people?" Christina asked.

"That's one of our city's biggest challenges, Christina," Mr. Jenkins replied. "We only receive about four inches of rain per year.

"Our major water source is the Colorado River," he continued, "and during periods of drought, it puts a strain on resources. To help provide more water, there's been talk of building a pipeline from the rural areas of Nevada to Las Vegas or even building a facility that would take ocean water and remove the salt."

"They'd have to remove the fish too!" Christina said, laughing.

"Well, at least the kids here don't have to go to school," Grant remarked.

"Why do you say that, Grant?" Mr. Jenkins asked.

"All I've seen in Las Vegas is bright lights and hotels," Grant said. "I haven't seen any schools."

"Aside from all the hotels and entertainment, Las Vegas is like any other community," Mr. Jenkins explained. "There are more than 180 elementary schools here in Clark County, more than 50 middle schools and more than 40 high schools."

"Wow, that's a lotta learnin'," an impressed Grant said.

While they laughed at Grant's observation, Christina noticed Asha and Chandu walk in the dining room. They looked very different wearing jeans and t-shirts.

"Good morning, Christina and Grant," Asha said. She looked tired, like she had not slept much the night before. "Good morning, Mr. Jenkins."

"These are our new friends, Asha and Chandu," Christina told Mimi and Papa. "They're from India and they're working with the tigers for Mr. Jenkins' show."

"*Were* working with the tigers," Asha corrected, her eyes filling with tears.

"Is there any news, Mr. Jenkins?" Chandu asked.

"I'm afraid not, kids," Mr. Jenkins replied. "It's a mystery why someone would want to take Soman and Shiba."

Christina let a big swallow of apple juice flow down her sore throat. *I wonder what happened to the tigers, she thought. As if there wasn't enough excitement in Las Vegas already, now they were knee-deep in a mystery!*

5 WHAT'S THAT NOISE?

Despite everyone's sad mood about the missing tigers, Papa was excited to get to the air show. He let Christina and Grant bring Asha and Chandu with them on the *Mystery Girl*.

Papa was not disappointed with Aviation Nation! The show included every size and shape of aircraft imaginable, even a Stealth bomber that Grant thought looked more like a spaceship than an airplane. Mimi lost her big red sun hat when a stunt plane swooped low and blew it right off her blond head.

"The *Mystery Girl* is the most beautiful plane here," Grant announced, as they settled back in Papa's aircraft for the return trip to Las Vegas.

"I agree," Papa said, flashing a big grin.

By the time the plane took off, the sun had set behind the purple desert mountains. Grant and Mimi found it was a good time for a nap.

The *Mystery Girl's* instruments cast a green glow around Papa's head. Outside the plane's windows, all was black. Christina saw no stars and no moon. She wondered how her grandfather knew which way was up or down! And worst of all, the desert below was filled with rattlesnakes, Gila monsters, horned lizards, and scorpions!

"I don't like flying at night!" Christina muttered.

"I think it's fun," said Chandu. "I've never been in a small plane before."

Christina noticed Asha staring out the window. "Are you OK?" she asked.

Asha shook her head. "I can't stop thinking about my tigers," she said. "Where can they be?"

"Don't worry," Christina said. "We're going to find out. Whoever took them must have left some type of clue."

Her train of thought was interrupted by a gurgling noise coming from Grant. He was sleeping in the shape of a pretzel with his skinny arms and legs crossed and blond head bobbing over the armrest. His mouth was open wide enough to catch flies and a drool stream trickled slowly down his chin.

This will be payback for some of those awful pictures he's made of me, Christina thought, quietly reaching for her camera. But she should have warned Papa and the snoozing Mimi. They both jumped when the flash lit the airplane cabin.

"What was that?" Mimi said, spinning around.

"Sorry, Mimi," Christina said, giggling. "Look—I couldn't resist that shot."

Mimi, Chandu, and Asha laughed too, as Grant continued his nap undisturbed.

When they finally stopped laughing, Christina asked, "Mimi, do you have any tissues up there?"

"Sure," Mimi answered.

As she reached for the tissue, an unusual sound interrupted the *Mystery Girl's* steady hum.

Mimi shot a worried look at Papa. Papa returned the look, but quickly said with a chuckle, "Maybe the *Mystery Girl* could use a tissue too."

Christina blew her stuffy nose and settled back into her seat. "Are you catching a cold?" Mimi asked.

"Las Vegas is too hot for me to have a cold!" Christina replied with a smile.

Suddenly, glittering color in the plane's windshield outlined dark mountains ahead and snatched the kids' attention.

"Look at that rainbow!" Christina said. "I've never seen one at night!"

"That's no rainbow," Mimi explained. "That's Las Vegas!"

"How much farther, Papa?" Christina asked. She couldn't wait to get back to Las Vegas!

Before Papa could answer Christina's question, the *Mystery Girl* let out an unmistakable sputter—and then another!

6 A BUMPY RIDE

The *Mystery Girl's* engine continued to skip noisily as Papa chatted anxiously with air traffic controllers at McCarran International Airport in Las Vegas. Christina and Asha instinctively squeezed their armrests.

"I'm not taking any chances," Papa yelled over the racket. "We're landing NOW!"

"Well, I did want to spend some time exploring the desert," Mimi said, with a nervous chuckle.

Sleeping soundly, Grant was unaware of the trouble. But just as Christina felt the plane start its descent, she noticed his unbuckled seatbelt. Without thinking, she unfastened hers and lunged over to buckle him up just as the plane became a roller coaster.

"Christina, what are you doing? Get back in your seat! NOW!" Mimi shrieked. Christina quickly buckled her seat belt and prepared for the rough landing.

"It's gonna be a bumpy ride, so brace yourselves!" Papa yelled, as he wrestled the controls.

WHAM!

The first bump was the worst. Without her seatbelt, Christina's head would have hit the plane's roof. The *Mystery Girl* became a bucking bronco as her wheels struggled to take hold in the desert sand. Finally, the bucking stopped. They were safely on the ground!

For several minutes, it seemed that everyone held their breath. Grant broke the silence. Stretching and yawning, he asked, "Hey, are we back in Las Vegas? It's sure a lot darker than I thought it would be." Everyone laughed, letting out the tension of the moment.

"We're about eight miles from Las Vegas," Papa answered. "We had to land a little sooner than I would have liked. The air traffic controllers are sending someone to pick us up in a helicopter. Would any of you like to stretch your legs while we wait?" He glanced at Mimi. "You might want to take off those red high heels, Missy," he suggested.

"Cool!" Grant said, unbuckling his seatbelt.

"Grant, do you realize there are scorpions out there?" Christina snapped.

"I know!" Grant exclaimed. "I was thinking we might catch one for a pet! Do you have anything we could keep it in 'til we get home?"

"Don't you realize scorpions can sting?" Christina asked. "Besides, they creep me out, just like spiders!"

"That may be because spiders and scorpions are both members of the arachnid family," Mimi explained. "Grant, please leave all the desert creatures in the desert! And all of you kids, put on your jackets! The desert gets cold at night, even in the summer."

Christina watched Papa and Grant step out first in the beams of the *Mystery Girl's* landing lights. When Christina looked out her side of the plane, a distant, shadowy figure with arms raised to the sky startled her. *Had their abrupt landing disturbed a desert dweller's rest?*

"Mimi, whaaaat's that?" Christina asked, her voice quivering.

"Oh, that's a Joshua tree," Mimi explained. "They got their name from the first Mormon settlers in this area who thought they looked like the Biblical prophet Joshua with his arms raised in prayer. Since Joshua trees can live to be 300 years old, that tree could have watched the first European explorers pass in the late 1700s!"

Her fears relieved, Christina's imagination raced as she remembered all she had read about the Mojave Desert that surrounds Las Vegas.

It was hard to believe where they sat was once a giant lake created by the melting glaciers of the Ice Age. As the lake slowly dried up, hunters of the Paleo Indian period had tracked mammoths and other large prehistoric animals on this same ground.

Much later, the Paiute Indians lived here for hundreds of years. Christina hoped they might see some of their petroglyphs, or ancient drawings on rocks, while they were here.

"Hey, look at this!" Grant shouted, lifting a dusty piece of knotted rope from the desert floor. "What is this thing?"

"Asha!" Chandu cried, grabbing the rope from Grant. "Look! It's Shiba's favorite toy!"

Asha raced to her brother's side to examine the discovery. "You're right!" she exclaimed. "What is it doing out here?"

Christina's mind began to race. *Had the tigers been out here in the desert? If so, why? And, where were they now?*

7 A ROYAL RESCUE!

A coyote's cry interrupted Christina's imaginary wanderings and spurred everyone back to the plane.

"That was enough 'leg-stretching' for me," Mimi remarked.

In a few minutes, Grant saw fast-moving lights skimming over sand and scruffy desert brush.

"We're rescued!" he exclaimed. He slapped Chandu's hand in a high-five, while Christina hugged Asha.

A mini sandstorm whipped up as the chopper landed. But as their rescuer got out and crossed into the *Mystery Girl's* landing lights, they could all see he was no ordinary man. His sequined suit glittered, and a shiny, red satin cape fluttered behind him!

When Papa opened the airplane's door, the dark-haired man curled his top lip and said, "I heard you folks might be *all shook up!*"

Grant and Christina were dumbfounded. Their rescuer was dressed like Elvis Presley!

"This is one crazy place," Papa murmured.

"Wow!" Grant yelled over the noise, as they buckled into their chopper seats. "I was excited about all the rides in Las Vegas. I didn't know I'd get a free helicopter ride too!"

Christina untangled her long brown hair after the chopper's rotors had swirled it around her head. She didn't share Grant's excitement.

"Great!" she murmured. "Another night-time flight!"

Elvis quickly handed out headsets. "Isn't that better than yelling?" he asked. "Welcome aboard *Cadillac*! I hope you enjoy your flight. We'll be back in Vegas in about 10 minutes."

As the chopper lifted from the desert floor, Christina watched Papa's concerned expression as the *Mystery Girl* got smaller and smaller. For him, leaving his beloved plane behind was like leaving a good friend.

"Do all the helicopter pilots in Vegas dress like Elvis?" Mimi asked. She patted her wispy blond hair back into place.

"You can see an Elvis **impersonator** doing almost everything in Las Vegas," he replied, "but I may be the only one who flies a helicopter."

"What's your real name?" Grant asked.

"My real name is Jack, but please call me Elvis," he said. "I grew up in Las Vegas, and I know this desert like the back of my hand. I give tours in *Cadillac* and rescue folks whenever the need arises. When I'm not doing that, I work at a couple of hotels impersonating 'The King.' Someday, I'd love to have my own show."

"You have a lot of jobs," Grant said.

"That's not all of them!" Elvis replied. "I also work for a sign company. When lights go out, they call me. The old neon signs are my specialty. I guess you could say I'm a 'jack of all trades'!"

"Do you kids know what neon signs are?" Mimi asked, always looking for educational moments.

"Neon lights work when an electric current is passed through a glass tube filled with neon gas," Christina answered. "I learned that in science class."

Elvis was impressed. "Christina," he said, "you know so much about neon, I'll have to recommend you for a job at the sign company! And speaking of lights, everyone take a look below at the 'Jewel of the Desert'!"

As the chopper rose above a ridge, Las Vegas sprawled before them like a tube of vivid glitter spilled on black construction paper. "It does look like a jewel!" Christina exclaimed, as the breathtaking, sparkling lights pierced the desert darkness.

Grant just stared, blue eyes wide and mouth gaping open.

In a moment, the chopper settled on the airport tarmac.

"I'm headed downtown in my van," Elvis remarked. "I'll be happy to give you folks a ride to your hotel."

"You all go ahead with Elvis," Papa said. "I'll see you there as soon as I find a good mechanic to take care of my plane."

"It looks like the fairgrounds!" Grant **observed**, as thousands of dancing, twinkling lights dazzled Mimi and the kids during the drive to the hotel.

"Yes," Mimi agreed, "except this fair never closes!"

Christina decided to tell Elvis about the missing tigers and showed him the rope toy they had found.

"A lot of things happen in Las Vegas," he cautioned, looking straight into Christina's eyes. "Always be alert to what's going on around you."

Elvis pulled his van to the curb so everyone could look down the famous Fremont Street. "If you'll look down there," he added, pointing like a tour guide, "you can see Vegas Vic—he's been welcoming visitors to Las Vegas since the 1940s."

"I don't see him," Grant whined.

"That's strange; he doesn't seem to be lit tonight," Elvis said. "I may get a call from the sign company about that!"

As soon as Elvis pulled up to the Mysteries Hotel, the children jumped out to inspect the magical fountain. Red, blue, and green blobs of water that shot from the fountain disappeared magically into the night sky, and then gently rained down into a pond as pastel drops.

"How does that work?" Grant asked, poking a curious finger into the shooting red liquid. But instead of going up, the colorful water spurted straight into Grant's face.

"Now your face matches your shirt," Christina observed, giggling.

"You're almost as entertaining as I am," Elvis told Grant.

"*Thank you, thank you very much* for the ride," Mimi said, in her best Elvis impression.

"Don't mention it, ma'am," Elvis replied.

"Will we see you again?" Christina asked.

Grabbing a pen and paper from his pocket, Elvis dashed off a note. "Here's my cell number. Maybe you can come to my act!"

As they watched Elvis drive away, Grant couldn't resist a corny comment. "Elvis has left the building!" he exclaimed.

"Good one," Mimi said, tousling Grant's blond curls.

But Christina wasn't thinking about corny jokes. *Why did Elvis look at me that way, she wondered. What do I need to watch out for in Las Vegas?*

8 NEON NIGHT

Christina and Grant said goodbye to Asha and Chandu and rode the elevator to their floor. Mimi stayed in the lobby briefly to speak to the concierge.

Christina stuffed her hand in her pocket for the card-key. When she pulled it out, everything else in her pocket came with it. There was the tissue the magician had given her the night before, the phone number from Elvis, and a sticky note she didn't recognize.

Unfolding it, she struggled to read sloppy handwriting that was not her own, or Grant's.

WHEN tHE COWBOY WaVeS, WatCH FOR tHE SiGNS.

"What's that?" Grant asked.

"I may have just found a clue," Christina answered. "But what does it mean?"

After Papa joined them for supper, Mimi said, "I know we've had a busy day, but would you kids like to stroll down Fremont Street before we go to bed?"

Christina cleared her throat. "Sure, Mimi," she answered hoarsely. "We couldn't see it very well when Elvis showed us from the car. But, could we stop for cough drops?"

"Sounds like you could use some," Mimi said.

Papa told the kids about Fremont Street as they walked. "You know, Fremont Street has been the main street of Las Vegas since it became a town," he said. "It became known as 'Glitter Gulch' after a lot of casinos were built here and their neon signs lit the night.

"Once the larger casinos were built on the strip," he continued, "nobody wanted to come to Fremont Street anymore. That's why they covered the street with a canopy that's like a movie screen for light shows. It's the largest screen on the planet—as long as five football fields!"

"What's the 'strip'?" Christina asked.

"It's the main road where most of the largest Las Vegas hotels are," Papa replied.

When they stepped under the Fremont Street canopy, the kids immediately saw how Glitter Gulch got its nickname. "It's so sparkly," Christina said, crunching the last bit of a cherry cough drop.

"I feel like I'm swimming in a bowl of my favorite breakfast cereal," Grant said, gazing in amazement at all the colors.

But, to their disappointment, the giant screen over the street was dark. "Awww," Grant complained. "I wanted to see the light show!"

Suddenly, the dark screen transformed into a bright blue daytime sky peppered with puffy white clouds.

Papa laughed as Grant instinctively ducked when a red airplane came out of nowhere and raced over their heads and down the screen. More planes chased the red plane, leaving behind trails of milky white smoke. In an instant, the sky changed again into a lush forest of trees swaying peacefully while the sound of chirping birds filled the air.

"Listen!" Mimi said. "I hear geese!"

A flock of gray geese with jet-black heads soared across the screen, followed by yellow hang gliders and colorful hot air balloons. A pounding tempo played in the background. When sky divers floated out of the sky, it was Christina's turn to duck as she was sure they were going to land on her head!

By the time a group of fighter jets zipped over their heads, Grant could resist the booming music no longer. He was dancing a jig as the screen's light turned him purple, green, and blue.

When the screen transformed into a night sky, a massive space shuttle launched into the stars. Christina watched until it disappeared and then looked down and rubbed her neck. "My neck hurts from looking up so much," she said.

"Well, why don't you look ahead," Mimi said. "There's Vegas Vic! And the cowgirl across the street is Vegas Vicki."

"He's lit up now!" Grant said, admiring Vic. "Do you think they called Elvis to fix him?" As they got closer, they noticed a huge crowd had gathered underneath the 50-foot-tall neon cowboy.

"What's going on?" Papa asked one of the gawkers.

"Vic is waving!" the man replied.

"Isn't he supposed to?" Papa asked.

"His arm hasn't moved for more than 15 years!" the man said. "It's been out of order. Someone has finally fixed it!"

"It was probably Elvis," Grant told the man.

Christina remembered the mysterious note she had found in her pocket.

Christina wondered if this could be what the note was describing. But...what signs? Surely the signs were clues. Clues to what?

9 CLUELESS IN THE CLOUDS

Christina and Grant knew there was still no news of the tigers' whereabouts as soon as they saw Asha's face the next day. Christina decided not to share the possible clue she had found until she knew more. She didn't want to get their hopes up. Still, she wanted to learn more about the mysterious white tigers.

"How did you get Soman and Shiba?" Christina asked.

"They were found in the wild after poachers shot their mother," Asha said.

"What are poachers?" Grant asked.

"They are bad men who kill wild animals and sell their body parts for money," Chandu explained.

"They have a great house here," Grant said, "but wouldn't Soman and Shiba have been happier in the jungle?"

"They could not have survived in the wild," Chandu answered. "Their color does not allow them to blend into their surroundings like normal orange Bengal tigers. Our father decided the best life for them would be here in this wonderful enclosure. He got to know Mr. Jenkins and learned he would take good care of the tigers. Mr. Jenkins also promised to donate some of the money from the show to tiger rescue operations in India. Did you know there are only about 3,000 Bengal tigers left in the wild?"

"Wow," Christina said. "I hope they don't become extinct!"

"Stink?" Grant asked. "Why would they start to stink?"

Chandu giggled. "She said 'extinct,' not 'stink,'" he explained. "To become extinct means that an animal species dies out completely."

"Well," Grant said, "I hope they don't become extinct—or stink!"

Asha continued, "Wild white tigers are very rare. Soman and Shiba are extra rare, maybe even magical."

"Because they're in a magic show?" Grant asked.

"No," Asha answered, "because they are twins, just like Chandu and me."

"OK, kids, it's time to explore the strip!" Papa announced, interrupting their conversation.

"Why don't you come with us?" Christina begged Asha and Chandu.

"No!" Chandu said. "We must stay here in case the tigers are returned."

Christina could tell there was no use arguing.

As Christina and Grant followed Mimi and Papa into the blinding sunshine, it suddenly occurred to Grant they might be exploring the wonders of Las Vegas on foot. "Papa, do we have to walk?" Grant whined.

Before Papa could answer, a huge yellow Hummer pulled up. It was as bright as the desert sunshine. Grant could hardly contain his excitement when he realized it was their ride.

"Sweeeeet!"

he exclaimed. "Papa, you really know how to cruise the Vegas strip in style!"

"Let's explore the north end of the strip first," Mimi said.

"Sounds like a plan!" Christina said, right before a sneeze.

"Christina, are you sure you feel all right?" Mimi asked.

"I feel much better today, Mimi," she replied. "I'm sure it's just allergies." Christina was not about to admit she had a cold and spoil the fun. Besides, she felt more excited than sick.

"Mimi, those buildings look like the ones we saw on our trip to Italy!" Grant observed, as they cruised past a magnificent hotel.

Before Mimi could comment, Christina explained, "That's the Venice Hotel, Grant. It's made to look like Italy and you can even ride gondolas there."

"Aren't those the boats driven by people with long poles?" Grant asked.

"Yes, Grant," Christina answered. "The people in the real Venice, Italy have used gondolas to ride around the canals for hundreds of years."

"I hope we get to ride one before we leave," Grant said. "I want to set a record on this trip for using different kinds of transportation!"

"Look at that!" Papa interrupted.

With so many things to look at, it was hard for Christina and Grant to know where to look. "Where?" Grant asked.

"Straight ahead," Papa said, seeing their confusion in his rear view mirror.

Out of the desert floor ahead of them rose a massive tower.

"I know what that is!" Grant announced. "That's the Stratosphere Hotel! It's the tallest building west of the Mississippi River!"

"Very good, Grant," Mimi said.

"I think that should be our first stop, since you can see everything from there," Grant said.

"The scariest rides in Las Vegas are there too!" Papa said. "Anyone game?"

"Are you kidding, Papa?" Christina said, assuring her grandfather she could handle any ride Las Vegas had to offer.

But as they pulled into the parking lot, Christina thought she might have to change her mind. As she looked up, she could see rides hanging over the side of the tower!

Inside the Stratosphere, Papa noticed one of the town's many casinos—where people try their luck at winning money.

"Look at all those one-armed bandits," Papa remarked.

"What's a 'one-armed bandit'?" Grant asked.

"It's a slot machine," Papa replied. "Grown-ups drop a coin in the slot to try and win *lots* of coins. They're called 'bandits' because they often take money but never give any back!"

"Why do people gamble if they can lose their money, Mimi?" Christina asked.

"Some people think of gambling as entertainment," Mimi explained. "It's fun and exciting to them, and they don't risk too much of their money. Most people gamble responsibly," she added, "but gambling can be a real problem for some people when they do it too much and lose an arm and a leg."

"Lose an arm and a leg?" Grant cried. "I'm never going to gamble if that's what happens!"

Papa chuckled. "No, Grant," he explained, "that expression means they might lose A LOT, like their home or their life savings."

"Look!" an excited Grant said, interrupting their conversation. "There's the ticket counter for the rides!"

Once Christina was strapped in the padded red vinyl harness of "The Big Shot" that would launch them all the way to the top of the tallest observation tower in the United States, she became nervous. I wish that Papa hadn't bought a package of tickets for all the rides at the Stratosphere, she thought. She glanced at Mimi and Papa, who looked as nervous as she felt.

"You scared?" she asked Grant, her white knuckles gripping the bars that held her in the seat.

"Me scared? You gotta be kidding!" he bragged.

As a man came around to make sure their harnesses were correctly fastened, Christina could imagine how astronauts feel! "Enjoy your ride!" was the last thing she heard before she shot into the sky.

Christina felt all the blood rush from her head as she closed her eyes.

When they stopped near the top of the tower, she opened her eyes to a breathtaking view of Las Vegas and the surrounding mountains. Above her, a few white puffy clouds looked close enough to touch.

She peeked at Grant, who still had his eyes closed. Before she could ask if he was ready to admit he was scared, Christina's hair shot straight up as they free-fell several hundred feet!

Christina screamed! She could hear Mimi screaming too.

"That was great!" Grant crowed, as they unbuckled. "Let's go ride the roller coaster. I've never ridden one on top of a building!"

The roller coaster was even more frightening. Not only did it have all the typical, stomach-churning twists and turns, but the view also reminded them just how far they were above the ground.

Christina was about ready to call it quits when Grant dragged Mimi and Papa to the Insanity ride.

"That's a perfect name for this ride!" Christina shouted, as a crane-like arm swung them over the side of the building in their little seats, before spinning them around like tops.

Thankful to have her feet on something solid when the ride was over, Christina wanted to keep them there. She had no desire to ride the X-Scream, a giant see-saw that made riders screech as they slid over the edge of the building, stopping just before being hurled over it!

"You all go ahead," Christina suggested, holding her head. Her face was the shade of green used for a witch's makeup on Halloween. "I think I'll sit this one out."

Watching her family being strapped into that ride was almost as scary as being on it herself. She had just said a quick prayer for their safety when two men standing nearby caught her attention. They were leaning against an overlook rail with their backs to her, having a heated argument. One was in a gray business suit, and the other wore a long black coat.

That's strange clothing for such a warm day, Christina thought. Also strange was what she could see at the bottom of the coat. The man was wearing sparkly blue pants just like those she had seen the magician wearing!

Christina could only hear bits and pieces of what the men were saying. The one thing she heard that stuck in her mind was the man in the suit telling Mr. Sparkly Pants, "Keep them in ice!"

What did that mean? Keep who, or what in ice? Did the man in the sparkly pants have something to do with the missing tigers?

10 A WALL OF CONCRETE

After another stomach-stretching visit to the buffet the next morning, Christina asked Asha and Chandu, "Have you ever visited Hoover Dam?"

"No," Asha answered. "We've heard about it, but we've been too busy since we got here."

"Well, I want you to come with us today!" Papa said.

"That's very kind of you, Mr. Papa," Asha said, "but we have to find Soman and Shiba."

Grant spewed his milk as he burst into laughter. "Mr. Papa! That's funny. I guess you're Mrs. Mimi," he said, pointing at his grandmother.

"I think those are great names for us," Mimi said, giving Grant a scolding look.

"Grant, no more milk showers, please," Christina said, wiping milk droplets from her arm.

"You kids shouldn't worry about Soman and Shiba," said Mr. Jenkins, who was having breakfast with them. "We'll let the police find their kidnappers."

"But they need special care!" Asha cried, upset again at the thought of her beloved tigers in the hands of strangers.

"Do you think they'll ask for a ransom, Mr. Jenkins?" Christina asked.

"I don't know, Christina. I haven't heard anything yet," Mr. Jenkins replied. "The only thing I know for sure is that if we don't find those tigers, we don't have a show."

With everyone looking downcast, Papa changed the subject.

"Hoover Dam will get our minds off our problems," he said.

"I heard men were buried alive in the cement at Hoover Dam," Grant remarked, "and their skeletons are still there!"

Cookie, the hotel cook, walked up as Grant was talking. "That story's been circulating since the dam was built, Grant," he said, "but have you ever heard the legend of the silver coin?"

"No!" Grant replied as he leaned forward to listen.

"One of the dam construction workers had come into Las Vegas and lost all the money from his paycheck in the casinos—except one silver coin," Cookie said.

"That's why I don't gamble," Grant interrupted. "I want to keep my arms and legs!"

"That's good, Grant," Cookie said. "Anyway, this construction worker was scheduled to return to his home in Kansas the next day. He was so ashamed he had lost his money that he threw his last coin over a railing at the dam, where it stuck in the wet cement. Legend has it that the person who sees the coin shining in the sun, pulls it from the cement, brings it back to Las Vegas, and puts it in a slot machine will win a huge jackpot!"

"That's certainly the coin I need to find!" Mr. Jenkins said, laughing. "That might solve all my money problems."

"Would you folks like me to make a sack lunch for you to take to the dam?" Cookie asked.

"That would be great, Cookie," Mimi replied.

"Are turkey sandwiches OK?" Cookie asked. "It's about all I have since someone stole 50 pounds of meat out of our freezer last night!"

"I don't need any more bad news, Cookie," Mr. Jenkins moaned.

When they all piled into the Hummer, Mimi went over her checklist. "Everyone buckled? Everyone have water bottles, sunscreen, sunglasses, and hats?" she asked.

"I don't like to wear sunglasses!" Grant protested.

"The desert sun can harm your eyes," Mimi said, slipping on her red, rhinestone-studded sunglasses. "In other words, you don't have a choice!"

During the 30-mile drive, all Chandu and Asha talked about were the missing tigers. Christina wanted to help her new friends solve their mystery, but she was also eager to see and learn about Hoover Dam, one of the top ten attractions for Las Vegas tourists. She tried to steer Chandu and Asha's thoughts away from the tigers.

"Mimi," Christina asked, "Hoover Dam was named for President Herbert Hoover, wasn't it?"

"That's right," Mimi replied, her blond hair blowing in the air conditioner breeze.

"What's the dam for, anyway?" Grant asked.

"The dam controls the flow of the Colorado River," Papa explained. "The river's power is used to make electricity for Nevada, California, and Arizona. The dam also created Lake Mead, which provides recreation and water for this desert region."

Papa turned to the window. "Start looking, kids, we're entering Black Canyon, home of Hoover Dam!"

"That's gi-normous!" Grant said, catching his first glimpse of the dam. "It looks like a giant wall of concrete with a big lake below it! I guess they need all that water to fill all those swimming pools in Las Vegas!"

After Papa bought the tickets for the Hoover Dam tour, they joined a small group standing near a uniformed guide.

"I am your guide to the magnificent Hoover Dam," the guide announced. "Welcome to one of the seven wonders of the industrial world! You are among a million guests who visit us each year."

Leading them through the giant structure, the guide explained that workers came from all over the country in 1931 to begin work on the dam. "Construction began during the Great Depression, and people needed jobs," he said. "Twenty-one thousand men helped build this dam. Let's watch a movie about how it was built."

Christina was glad to slip into the cool, dark theater. During the movie, the kids learned that the 54-story dam contained enough concrete to build a two-lane highway from San Francisco to New York—all the way across the United States!

When the movie was over, the guide asked for questions. Christina knew what was coming. Grant's hand shot into the air.

"How many men are buried in the cement?" he asked.

"There are none," the guide answered. "There were 114 men who died during construction from falling off the dam or canyon walls, being hit by falling rock, and other accidents. But no one was buried in the concrete."

That's one huge dam!

"Oh," Grant said, a bit disappointed.

Looking at the giant red and silver generators quickly changed Grant's mood. Seeing the powerful humming machines making electricity, Grant said, "I feel like I'm in the engine room of a giant spaceship!" He pretended to have a headset on, and began barking orders to his imaginary crew.

After the tour, the kids wanted one more look from the top of the dam. The Colorado River boiled angrily at the dam base, but then flowed like blue ribbon between the rocky, brown canyon walls.

As Mimi and Papa read a plaque about those who lost their lives during the construction, the kids watched the churning water below.

Christina was about to show Asha a little rainbow that had formed in the frothy spray above the water, but Asha was no longer beside her. "Asha!" Christina called. "Where are you?"

Christina grabbed Grant and Chandu. "Asha is missing," she said. "Do either of you know where she is?"

Both boys shrugged their shoulders. "We were too busy trying to make echoes," Grant said.

"Well, let's start looking," Christina suggested. "You two go to the right, and I'll go to the left."

Christina darted in and out of groups of tourists, looking for her friend, dressed in a lime green top and blue jeans. Suddenly, she saw a flash of green between two round towers. There was Asha—and it looked like she was jumping back and forth!

Christina called the boys to follow her and ran over to Asha. "What are you doing?" Christina asked, out of breath.

"I'm jumping from one time zone to another!" Asha exclaimed. "This line here separates the Mountain Time Zone from the Pacific Time Zone. If you stand in Mountain Time, it's two o'clock. If you stand in Pacific Time, it's only one o'clock!"

"So," said Grant, "if I have one foot on each side of the line, does that make it 1:30?" Chandu giggled at Grant's joke.

"That's so cool," Christina remarked. She noticed two large clocks depicting the correct time in Nevada and in Arizona. "Now that's a good way to turn back time!"

"It's funny you say that," Asha remarked, suddenly looking sad. "I was wishing I could turn back time to before Soman and Shiba disappeared. Maybe then I could do something to prevent it from happening."

Christina put her arm around Asha's shoulders. "I know," she said, "let's just keep our eyes and ears open! There have got to be clues out there to help us find out what happened to them!"

"KIDS!" Papa's booming voice startled everyone, including nearby tourists. "It's time to go!"

Grant put his hand on his chin like he was pondering something very important. "So," he said, "how do we really know it's time to go? Is Papa in Mountain Time or Pacific Time?"

Christina pushed Grant in front of her. "Nice try," she said, "but when Papa says it's time to go, it's time to go!"

11 FROM THE MEADOWS

During the return trip from Hoover Dam, Christina decided to tell Asha and Chandu about possible clues she had so far.

"I'm not sure what it all means," Christina said. "But I think we should keep our eyes open and watch for the signs now that Vegas Vic is waving again. Unfortunately, I'm not sure what kind of signs."

Christina folded her arms and looked out the Hummer's window. "Let's think like kidnappers," she said. "Where would you hide white tigers in Vegas?"

"You can't put tigers just anywhere," Asha said, "especially white ones."

Grant had an idea. "How about The Secret Garden of Siegfried and Roy?" he asked. "They already have white tigers there. Wouldn't that be a perfect place for the kidnappers to hide more?"

"That's certainly a good place to start, Grant," Chandu said. "Do you think Mr. Papa would take us there?"

Grant giggled again at Papa's new courtesy title. "Of course he will," Grant answered. "Watch this."

In his best "sweet little grandson" voice, Grant asked, "Papa, it's still early. Could you take us to The Secret Garden of Siegfried and Roy?"

"Sure," Papa answered, "but I want to ride the monorail. It goes to the Mirage, near the Secret Garden. How does that sound?"

"Great!" Grant answered for everyone else. "That'll be another mode of transportation I can add to my list!"

"I'm loving this!" Grant cried, as the monorail zipped along raised tracks past the glittering Vegas hotels. "I wish I could stick my head out the window!"

Christina nodded. "I feel like I've been transported to the future!"

The Secret Garden was a much larger version of the tigers' enclosure at the Mysteries Hotel. As the children walked through the lush, green landscape, Chandu said, "This reminds me of the jungles of India."

Christina's heart skipped a beat when she caught a glimpse of white ahead. "Look!" she shouted. The kids left Mimi and Papa behind as they ran ahead to investigate.

To their dismay, the flash of white did not belong to tigers, but to white lions with shaggy white manes. "Where are the white tigers?" Christina asked an employee emptying a trash can.

"Next enclosure," he answered. "Just got some new ones."

That was exciting news!

Asha and Chandu **scrutinized** all the tigers. "A tiger's stripes are like fingerprints," Chandu explained. "No two are the same."

"I don't see them," Asha said, disappointed.

Just to make sure, Chandu called out, "Soman! Shiba!" The only response he received were puzzled looks from passersby.

The next small enclosure included two small white tiger cubs. Park attendants allowed guests to come in and pet them. "Cool!" Grant exclaimed. "I want to pet the baby albino tigers!"

"They are not albinos," Chandu corrected. "They are white tigers. They just don't have the usual orange pigment in their fur."

As they stroked the cubs' thick white fur, Christina was shocked that it felt rough, not soft like the fur of a house cat. Petting the cubs only made Asha and Chandu long for their own tigers.

When Mimi and Papa caught up, they could see the kids' sad expressions. "The police will find your tigers," Mimi told Chandu and Asha.

"But will they find them in time for opening night, Mrs. Mimi?" Asha asked.

"I hope so, Asha," Mimi said, stroking Asha's glossy black hair.

"Would you all like to make one more stop before we head back to the hotel?" Papa asked, trying to lighten the mood again. "We could take a trolley ride to Madame Tussauds."

"Is that another one of your old friends, Papa?" Grant asked.

"No, she certainly is not!" Papa said, chuckling. "Madame Tussauds is a wax museum."

"Gross!" Grant exclaimed. "Who wants to look at a bunch of old ear wax?"

"Grant, it's not ear wax!" Christina said. "They use a special kind of wax to make models of famous people. You'll see!"

"Well, at least I'll get to ride the trolley," Grant said. "You know I'm making a list—"

"We know!" they all said before he could finish.

If the monorail felt like the future, the trolley felt like the past. As they poked along, the sky was growing dark and the bright lights of Las Vegas were beginning to sparkle.

"This would be a good time to watch for the signs," Christina suggested. She pulled out her digital camera and began taking a picture of every sign they passed.

The first thing Christina noticed when they arrived at the Madame Tussauds was a sign advertising a new exhibit.

Was this a sign they should be watching for? Christina hoped not. She knew the tigers in this display would not be living. But she also wondered if the artists had to have tiger skins to stretch over the wax forms!

Inside the museum, Christina was amazed at how real the wax figures were! Mimi made a beeline to the wax version of Elvis.

Snapping pictures and looking for signs!

"Christina, take my picture with Elvis," Mimi said. "I can't believe I'm standing next to the King!"

Papa headed straight for the likeness of his golf hero, Tiger Woods. "What did you shoot today, old buddy?" he asked the wax statue, like they were old pals!

Christina didn't think the others had noticed the tiger display sign and she wanted to check it out alone—just in case her worst fears were true. Finding the skins of their beloved tigers stretched over wax figures was the last thing Asha and Chandu needed!

As the others visited their favorite wax celebrities, Christina slipped behind a partition and into the tiger display room. She found an artist adding the finishing touches to the display.

"I'm sorry, but this display is not open yet," the artist said.

"Oh, I'm sorry," Christina said. "They sure are beautiful," she continued, carefully eyeing the tigers. "I guess those are real tiger skins."

"Of course not," the artist said. "They are fake fur. We'd never kill tigers for their skins!" Christina breathed a sigh of relief. Now I can relax and enjoy the museum, she thought, skipping over to join the other kids.

Back at the hotel, the children looked at the pictures Christina had made during their outing. She had some good shots from Hoover Dam, but what caught Christina's attention were the pictures of signs she had taken from the trolley.

"Grant, bring me paper and a pen," she ordered.

"What do you see?" Asha asked.

"A lot of these signs have letters missing!" Christina said.

"That just means someone needs to change the bulbs," Grant remarked, unimpressed.

"But what if those missing letters spell out a clue?" Christina asked.

She jotted down the missing letters in the order the pictures were taken as they traveled down the strip. "Hey! It spells something!"

"What could that mean?" Chandu asked.

"Wait a minute!" Grant said. He bolted to his nightstand and grabbed his Las Vegas guidebook.

"I saw something like that in here," he said, flipping pages. "Here it is! 'The Meadows' was the original name for Las Vegas. Spanish traders named it after they found springs of water here."

"Grant, that's it!" Christina said, pleased with her brother's discovery. "Soman and Shiba have been taken 'from the Meadows'—from Las Vegas!"

12 MORE MEAT EATERS

"Any news from the police?" Papa asked Mr. Jenkins the next morning.

"Nothing yet," he replied. "Our big opening is only two days away. I guess I need to cancel it."

"I wouldn't cancel anything yet," Christina said. "You never know what may happen today!"

"Thanks for the encouragement, Christina," Mr. Jenkins said. "Maybe we will have good news today."

"Is everyone ready for the day's adventures?" Mimi asked. She was ready for sightseeing in the desert sun with her wide-brimmed straw hat adorned with a bright red bow.

"Where are we going today?" Christina asked, wiping her nose.

"I thought we could check out the Shark Reef at Mandalay Bay and the Adventure Dome," Mimi said.

"I think I'd rather stay at the hotel today and wait for news of the tigers," Asha said.

"You have to go with us!" Christina demanded. Dropping her voice to a whisper she said, "Do you really think clues are gonna walk in here and tap you on the shoulder?"

"You're right," Asha agreed.

Grant whirled around, with a twinkle in his eye. "Since we're in the desert," he said, "I guess we're going to see sand sharks! Get it— sand sharks?!" His joke got a little giggle out of Asha.

As they drove past the magnificent Excalibur Hotel, Christina thought it looked like the perfect fairytale castle. It made Grant think of something else.

"Gotta go!" Grant announced.

"You're kidding!" Mimi said, annoyed. "We just left the hotel."

"Sorry, Mimi, but I gotta go now!" Grant repeated.

Papa whipped the Hummer into the Excalibur parking lot. "I'll wait here. Maybe you should all take a tour of the bathrooms!"

A tall, skinny man with a long white beard, a pointed hat, and dark, flowing robes greeted them inside.

"Which way to the bathroom?" Grant asked.

"Follow the enchanted trail," the mysterious man answered, pointing ahead. "Tell them Merlin sent you."

"Thanks!" Grant said. "I've never had a magician give me bathroom directions before!"

Chandu and Grant headed in one direction and the girls in another. When the girls returned to the entrance, there was no sign of Grant and Chandu, but they did see a knight in clanking armor and a stunning damsel in a pink gown.

"Think we'll see Prince Charming?" Christina asked Asha. In a moment, Grant and Chandu ran up, huffing and puffing.

"Sorry!" Grant said. "Somehow we made a wrong turn and wound up in a jousting arena. A knight on a big, black horse almost ran over me!"

"Maybe the horse was in a hurry to find the bathroom, too!" Christina said, shaking her head. "Let's go see the sharks!"

At the Shark Reef, workers fed huge hunks of raw meat to the rare golden crocodiles. "That's disgusting!" Christina said. Asha didn't say anything but the expression on her face told that she agreed.

"They swallow that whole!" Grant said, clearly fascinated.

"Yeah, that's so cool!" Chandu agreed.

Mimi had seen enough. "Let's get inside out of this heat," she said. A cool, dark tunnel led them to the aquarium where dazzling tropical fish darted, eels slithered, and sharks prowled above their heads.

As Christina watched the creatures, her thoughts slowly drifted back outside to the crocodiles and the hunks of meat. She remembered Cookie's report about the meat stolen from the hotel freezers. *Wouldn't the people who stole the tigers need meat to feed them?*

13 CIRCUS CLUES

"Mimi, I've been in this desert sun too long!" Grant said on the way to Adventuredome at the Circus, Circus resort. "I think I'm hallucinating!"

"Why do you think that, Grant?" Mimi asked.

"Because I see blue people walking down the sidewalk!" Grant replied.

"Oh, that's the Blue Man Group!" Christina exclaimed. "I wish we had time to see their show."

"What do they do?" Grant asked. "Wrestle in blueberries?"

"They're entertainers, who never speak, but tell stories with props and drums," Christina explained. "I had a friend in school who sat in the front row at a show and left covered with bits of smashed tomatoes!"

"Yessss! That sounds like my kind of show!" Grant shouted.

Talking about tomatoes reminded Christina to share her tiger food theory with Asha and Chandu. "Who would be able to steal meat from the hotel?" she asked.

"It would have to be someone who has a key to the kitchen storage area," Chandu answered. "Hey! They would probably have a key to the storage area where we were locked up too!"

As they entered the massive glass dome of Adventuredome, a startled Asha jumped when Sparkles the clown yelled, "Welcome to my circus!" Christina was overwhelmed by the flashing lights and size of the place, but immediately noticed signs with burned-out letters.

"It looks like our clue man has been at work here," she said. She reached for her camera, but realized when she pressed the shutter that her memory card was full. She jotted down the letters instead.

"This is the largest indoor theme park in the country," Mimi said. "I want you kids to enjoy it. You don't have to stay with Papa and me, but please stay together!"

As exciting as the rides and games looked, the kids were more interested in gathering letters. So far, Christina had found four letters:

HNEW. For an experienced clue decoder, that one was easy. "'WHEN'," she said with certainty.

Watching the Sling Shot launch riders 100 feet into the air, Chandu noticed a sign describing the ride with the entire word RISES unlit.

"Do you think that's part of a clue?" he asked, trying to be heard above the screams.

"I'm writing it down," Christina said. "WHEN and RISES. Now all we need is a subject for the sentence."

"That's right," Grant agreed, slurping a snow cone that was turning his lips and tongue blue. "A person, place, or thing, that's what we need."

Asha, who was also getting into the hang of looking for clues, spotted the next unlit word, THE, in a sign for Xtreme Zone, where people were rock climbing and bungee jumping.

Christina read what she had so far. "WHEN THE *blank* RISES. OK, guys, I think we only need one more word and we'll know where to go next," Christina said.

Grant was tired of looking for clues. "Can't we do something fun?" he asked. "Let's play a round of miniature golf."

Grant soon regretted his choice as the other kids quickly racked up better scores than he did. The final straw came when he hit a golf ball that bounced off a fake palm tree, hit a tourist in a Hawaiian shirt smack on his bottom, and splashed into a small pond. When the man looked around to see where the ball came from, the giggling kids quickly looked the other way.

When the irritated tourist gave up on finding his attacker and walked away, Christina saw Grant pull off his shoes.

"What are you doing?" she asked.

"You don't want me to get my shoes wet when I wade in after my golf ball, do you?" he asked.

"Grant! You can't do that!" Christina yelled as Grant ran for the water. But when she got to the pond, she was glad he hadn't listened. In front of her was the missing word for their clue!

"BEWARE OF THE WATER HAZARD" a sign read. But the word WATER was unlit.

"Grant, you're a genius!" Christina said. She wrote the clue on her paper:

When the Water rises

"Now, all we have to do is figure out what it means," Christina murmured.

Suddenly, the kids heard familiar voices.

"Look at these scaredy cats!" Mimi said. "While we've been riding roller coasters, they've had a quiet game of miniature golf!"

14 SPIKES AND THE SPHINX

"How about a snack?" Mimi asked as Papa wove the Hummer through a steady stream of cars and limousines on the strip.

"What do you have in mind?" Papa asked.

"I'd really like to sample some chocolate at the Ethel M Chocolate Factory," Mimi answered. "They also have a cactus garden there."

"Chocolate and cactus?" Christina said. "That's the weirdest combo I've ever heard of."

"Not really," Mimi explained. "The owner, Frank Mars, loved growing cacti. And I guess you could say he was a 'stickler' for chocolate."

"Mimi, I would expect a corny joke like that from Grant, but not from you," Christina said with a giggle.

When they entered the factory, the kids were overwhelmed with a familiar scent.

"Oh, this smells like chocolate heaven," Asha said.

"It's like falling into a cup of Mimi's cocoa," Grant raved after taking a long, deep sniff.

"I can't smell anything with this stuffy nose!" Christina whined. "I sure hope I'll be able to taste it."

Walking along a glass window, they watched giant pots of warm pecan brittle poured onto tables, then rolled into shiny gold sheets.

In one kitchen, a lady cooked candy centers, and then sent them "naked" to the next room to be clothed in rich, velvety chocolate. Another chocolatier made green apples look like balls of yarn as he drizzled silky white and dark chocolate over them. In the factory's last room, workers dressed sweet treats in red, green, and blue foil. "They look like Christmas ornaments," Grant observed.

Exiting into the Chocolate Shoppe, each of them chose a free sample. "I wish I could dip you in chocolate, Grant," Christina said. "You'd be so much sweeter."

"I'm already sweeter than you," her brother fired back.

"Are not!"

"Am too!"

Amused, Asha and Chandu watched their friends bicker. But their minds were somewhere else. In the cactus garden, they pulled Christina aside as Mimi, Grant, and Papa admired a tall cactus that looked like it needed a shave.

"We're wasting time," Chandu said. "We have to find out where the water rises!"

"Just keep your eyes and ears open!" Christina told him. "You never know where you'll find a mystery clue!"

"I never knew there were so many different kinds of cacti," Asha said, as they strolled along the winding paths. "I like the ones with the flowers blooming on them."

"That one has gray hair," Chandu said, pointing at a squatty cactus covered with white spines that resembled hair. "The sign says it's an 'old man' cactus and the hair helps protect it from the sun."

"Cactus stickers also help protect them from thirsty animals that want to get to the water they store inside," Christina added.

Stopping to look at a saguaro cactus pointing at the sky, Christina heard two young couples chatting about Las Vegas. When one of the women said, "The sphinx's eyes make the lake rise," Christina knew she was hearing something important! But before she could hear more, something snatched everyone's attention.

YEEEOWWWWW!!!

Park attendants rushed past Christina to find out who was yelling. She was not surprised to see her red-faced brother being rescued from a large cactus that looked like a man with dreadlocks.

"Grant!" Mimi cried. "Are you all right?"

"Yes, ma'am," Grant answered. "Those cactus things just grab me like a magnet everywhere I go! I'll never be able to drink water again. I'm full of holes!"

As Mimi followed Grant to the bathroom to help him pick the stickers from his backside, Christina looked for the people who were talking about the sphinx. They were gone! But she figured there was only one place they could be talking about—Egypt in Las Vegas—the Luxor Hotel!

Back in the Hummer, Grant perched gingerly on the edge of his seat. "I think we missed a sticker, Mimi," he said.

"Papa, will we pass Egypt?" Christina asked. "I mean, the Luxor Hotel?"

"I think so," Papa replied.

"Could we please stop there?" Christina begged.

"If that's what everyone else wants to do," Papa said. Christina had told Asha and Chandu about the sphinx and the lake. "Yes, please, Mr. Papa!" they chimed.

At the Luxor Hotel, the kids were **mesmerized** as the green laser-beam from the Great Sphinx's eyes hit the lake. First, it boiled. Then, like magic, it rose in a curtain of water and became a movie screen showing pictures of ancient Egypt.

"This is so cool," Christina said. "But what does it have to do with the tigers?"

"Maybe that clue was just to get us here," Chandu offered. "We should go inside."

Inside the pyramid-shaped hotel, they made a beeline to the most interesting thing they saw— King Tut's tomb. It was a replica of the young boy-king's burial chambers that archaeologist Howard Carter discovered in 1922.

"Watch it!" Christina snapped at Grant as he bumped into her in the dimly lit chamber filled with mummies and artifacts. "These mummies give me the creeps! "Look how bright that is," she said. Christina pointed to some spotlighted hieroglyphics.

A tour guide noticed their interest. "Did you know that King Tut was forced to marry his half-sister?" he asked. "This depicts that wedding."

"Yuck!" Grant said without hesitation. "That poor guy!"

Leaving the tomb, Christina felt like she was trying to put together a jigsaw puzzle without the picture on the box. If the wedding scene really was a clue, she couldn't imagine how it fit in the picture!

Asha looked just as confused and hopeless. Looking at her watch, she said, "Thirty-six hours until the show!"

15 A NATURAL CLUE

"The old girl is running better than ever!" Papa exclaimed, as he hung up the phone. "The mechanic said the *Mystery Girl* is ready and waiting for us."

"Kids," Mimi said, "this is our last day of Vegas sight-seeing. What would you like to do?"

"I've just GOT to see those robot dinosaurs at the Las Vegas Natural History Museum," Grant said.

"And I've just GOT to dig for fossils there," Christina added. She figured that dinosaurs would be just the thing to distract Chandu and Asha from their worries.

At the museum, the dinosaurs did more than distract the twins. The ancient monsters terrified Asha, who peered at them while hiding behind Christina.

"If these guys had been in the desert a few days ago, we would have never made it to Las Vegas!" Christina told Grant.

On the way to the Museum Discovery Room to dig for fossils, another display caught Christina's eye. It was about a natural formation near Las Vegas called Ice Box Canyon.

Why does that sound familiar, Christina wondered. As she read about the shady canyon's vegetation and waterfalls, her memory provided the answer. It was the men at the Stratosphere saying, "Keep them in ice!"

Her mind was racing. If they had deciphered the clues correctly, the tigers were not in Las Vegas. *Could they be in Ice Box Canyon? Maybe Shiba's toy had been dropped in the desert on the way there!* Christina knew it was a stretch. But solving mysteries had taught her one important thing—to trust her own instincts.

With time for only one more sightseeing stop, Christina knew what her choice would be!

16 COOL CANYON

"I've never been so hot in my life!" Grant whined, wiping the sweat running like rivers down his flushed face. "I wish I had a freezer pop the size of this rock!" he continued, picking up a jagged stone and tossing it into the sand.

Suddenly, the kids could hear a loud hissing sound like the air being let out of a tire. Grant's rock had been the roof of a Gila monster's home!

"Look how colorful he is," Grant said, admiring the chubby lizard's orange and black splotches. "His skin looks like shiny little beads."

"Grant, don't move," a terrified Christina warned. "They're poisonous!"

"He can't bite me, I'm wearing boots!" Grant answered, easing in for a closer look at the two-foot long creature.

Grant's motion sent the Gila monster scurrying for cover, right over the top of Christina's foot, which was covered only by thin sandal straps.

Mimi and Papa bolted over when they heard Christina scream.

"Grant!" Christina yelled. "That thing could have bitten me!"

"She's right, Grant," Mimi scolded. "Gila monsters bite their prey and poison from the mouth goes into the wound. Fortunately, they prefer small mammals to big sisters!" Mimi said as she gave Christina a big squeeze.

"Don't pick up any more rocks, Grant!" Christina ordered. "I'm not kidding!"

Walking farther into the canyon, Christina could feel the temperature slowly drop as the canyon walls began to shade the canyon floor.

"That feels great!" Grant said. "It feels like standing in a refrigerator."

"Ice box," Christina suggested.

"Listen!" Grant said. "Now it sounds like someone's pouring a glass of water from the refrigerator."

"Ice box," Christina said again.

"Hey, I think I hear a stream," Chandu said, running ahead.

When the other kids caught up, leaving Mimi and Papa behind, Chandu was hopping from rock to rock across the cold, crystal-clear water. When he reached the other side, he stopped in his tracks, almost losing his balance on a rock.

"Bones!" he yelled.

Bones! Bones! Bones! The word echoed off the canyon walls and in Christina's head.

Were they too late? Had the tigers been killed here? Had their valuable skins and body parts already been sold?

When Papa and Mimi caught up, Grant was turning a bone over in his hand.

"What kind are they, Papa?" he asked.

"I have no idea how they got here, but it looks like they came from a side of beef," Papa replied.

"This has to be the beef stolen from the hotel!" Christina whispered to Asha and Chandu. "The tigers were here!"

"But where are they now?" Asha asked.

A passing hiker interrupted their conversation. "Have you folks found something interesting?" he asked, eyeing the bones. "I certainly saw something interesting about an hour ago."

"What?" Christina asked.

"A helicopter was lifting a big old crate straight up out of the canyon," the hiker said. "You don't see that every day!"

Without hesitation, Christina shouted, "Papa, we've got to get back to Las Vegas—NOW!"

Don't lose your balance!

17 SIGNS OF HELP

Papa struggled to hurry in the congested, rush-hour traffic on the Strip. Christina, who had shared everything she knew with Mimi and Papa, gave everyone their assignments.

Grant was to search in his guidebook for helicopter pad locations in Vegas. Asha and Mimi were to scour the left side of the strip for possible clues. Christina and Chandu were to look on the right side.

"Find anything, Grant?" Christina asked.

"Nothing yet," was the disappointing reply.

"Got a G!" Mimi said excitedly, her mystery-solving instincts now in full gear as she spotted the burned-out letter on a neon sign.

Asha hit the next jackpot. "OING," she said. "I haven't learned that English word yet," she added.

"That's not a word by itself," Christina said. "But if you put the G in front of it, you've got GOING!"

"I don't believe this!" Grant said. "Did you know they have helicopter weddings here?"

"You're supposed to look for helicopter pads, not weddings!" Christina scolded. Then, she slowly turned toward her brother with an 'I've got an idea!' look on her face.

"Remember those hieroglyphics at King Tut's Tomb?" she asked. "The one about the wedding? Could a wedding be part of this mystery?"

Before she could answer her own question, Chandu shouted, "You missed it! I saw the word TO—it was unlit!"

"Sorry, Chandu," Christina said. "I'll pay attention." Her attention paid off in a few minutes as they passed a sign with THE unlit.

Christina repeated what they had so far. "GOING TO THE blank!"

"CHAPEL!" Asha yelled as they passed the Little White Chapel.

"Very good, Asha!" Mimi praised. "I didn't even notice that one."

"If our clue is correct, they're taking the tigers to a chapel!" Christina said.

"There are so many chapels in Vegas," Chandu said. "How would we know which one?"

Grant suddenly tapped his guidebook. "It could be Paradise Falls," he suggested. "There's a helicopter pad not far from that one!"

18 GOIN' TO THE CHAPEL

"Papa, why aren't we moving anymore?" Christina asked impatiently.

"There's a fender-bender ahead," he answered.

As she watched Asha bite her nails and Chandu rocked nervously, Christina couldn't take it any longer. "We should run the rest of the way," she blurted out.

"Oh, no, you don't!" Mimi said.

"Mimi, we'll all stay together," Christina pleaded. "I have my cell phone, and I can call you if we need anything! Plus, you'll be right behind us!"

"Is that Elvis?" Grant asked, spying the familiar hair and costume.

"You know Elvis is everywhere in Las Vegas, Grant!" Christina said.

But Grant had already rolled down his window and yelled, "Hey, Elvis!"

Elvis glanced and gave a quick wave. Then he did a double-take, recognizing the kids. This wasn't any Elvis. It was their Elvis—the desert rescuer.

"What are you kids doing?" Elvis asked.

"Elvis, do you know the way to Paradise Falls Wedding Chapel?" Christina shouted.

"Sure!" Elvis replied. "I sing for weddings there sometimes. You plannin' on getting married tonight, darlin'?" he asked in his best Elvis voice.

Christina had barely finished explaining about the tigers when Chandu blurted, "Will you please take us there, Mr. Elvis?"

"Is that all right with you folks?" Elvis asked Mimi and Papa.

"Well, it looks like we're not going to get there anytime soon," Papa answered. "Go ahead."

"Let's go this way," Elvis motioned. Racing like a superhero through the crowds, his red-lined cape rippled like a flag to guide them.

"Lucky thing we ran into Elvis!" Grant cried.

"No kidding!" Christina said, concentrating on the cape. But the more Christina thought about their lucky meeting with Elvis, the more her suspicions grew.

Hadn't Elvis told them he repaired lights for a sign company? And hadn't all the clues had to do with lights? Weren't the tigers pulled from Ice Box Canyon by a helicopter? And didn't Elvis fly a helicopter? And why didn't he seem surprised when Christina told him about the kidnapped tigers?

Was Elvis the kidnapper leading them on a wild goose chase away from the tigers instead of to them? There were just too many coincidences!

Christina suddenly stopped. "What are you doing?" Asha shouted. "We'll lose him!"

Christina motioned for the kids to follow her into a nearby gift shop, where she shared her fears about Elvis.

"Something about him does remind me of one of the men who locked us up," Chandu said.

"But how will we find Paradise Falls now?" Asha asked.

A deep voice interrupted. "May I help you?" the store clerk asked.

"Yes!" Christina said, urgently asking for the directions they needed.

"Sure," he answered. "You'll find it at the Flamingo Hotel."

The kids resumed their race along the Vegas strip. Grant looked up as they passed the Eiffel Tower at the Paris Las Vegas Hotel. "I feel like I've run halfway around the world!" he said, breathless from running.

"You have—in a magical, Las Vegas sort of way," Christina replied.

At the Flamingo, Christina could see the frustrated Elvis waiting out front. "We can't go in that way!" Christina commanded. "Let's find a back way into the hotel."

Running frantically down the strip again, Grant stopped suddenly, causing a pileup as Chandu and Asha crashed into him. The flames and spewing lava of an erupting volcano at the Mirage Hotel had stolen his complete attention.

"It's not real, Grant!" Christina shouted. "Get moving!"

Their next obstacle was the canal at the Venetian Hotel.

"How will we get across?" Chandu asked.

"I see an empty gondola!" Grant answered. "Anybody know how to drive this thing?" he asked, as the kids climbed into the narrow boat.

"I guess we will figure it out!" Christina exclaimed, grabbing the long pole at the back of the boat. "I need some help!" she ordered.

Everyone balanced around her, grabbed the pole, and pushed as hard as they could. They were gliding across the canal!

As they pulled up to the other side, however, an angry voice startled them. "What are you kids doing?" Elvis yelled. "We don't have time for this!"

"He must have seen us and followed us here!" Christina cried. With nowhere to run, Christina could no longer hold in her suspicions. "Did you help steal the tigers?" she shouted.

"There's no time to explain," Elvis answered. "If you want to see those tigers again, get out of that boat and follow me!"

Was Christina wrong about Elvis? Still unsure what was going on, they had to take a chance. The show was set to begin in a couple of hours.

"Let's go with him," Christina said to the kids. They scrambled out of the gondola onto dry land.

Christina pulled out her cell phone and called Mimi. "Meet us at the Flamingo," she whispered, so Elvis wouldn't hear. "With the police!"

19 ROYAL WEDDING

Peeking from behind a clump of palm trees at Paradise Falls, the kids couldn't believe their eyes. A red carpet path led to a robed minister waiting in front of a rocky waterfall. On each side, lush foliage and vivid flower arrangements framed a leafy altar. Lights and cameras surrounded the scene.

"What's going on?" Grant whispered.

"It looks like a wedding!" Christina answered.

Suddenly, jungle drums overwhelmed the peaceful rush of the waterfall and an organ joined the beat to play a wedding march.

At the opposite end of the red carpet, a man in a blue sparkly outfit caught Christina's eye. As he stepped onto the carpet, the kids gasped. He was leading a pair of growling, hissing, white tigers!

"That's Soman and Shiba," Asha whispered. "I'm sure of it!"

"Yes, and that's Manendra, the magician," Chandu said.

A deep, booming voice drew the kids' attention to the other side of the waterfall. "From the jungles of India...they have come to Las Vegas to be King and Queen of the Strip!"

"Why are they doing this?" Christina whispered to Elvis.

"It's a big publicity stunt," Elvis whispered back. "See that man in the gray business suit? He's also opening a big magic show at his new resort. I guess he decided the quickest way to get white tigers was to steal them!"

"Does anyone object to these magnificent creatures becoming our King and Queen?" the announcer asked.

To Christina's horror, Asha jumped out from behind the palm trees. "I do!" she yelled. "Soman, Shiba come!"

Hearing Asha's voice, Soman bared his claws and slapped Manendra's leg. When the startled magician grabbed his leg in pain, Soman and Shiba stripped their leashes from his hands.

SMASH!

CRASH!

The tranquil tropical scene became chaos as the tigers galloped towards Asha, knocking over cameras and scattering people in their path.

"Hold it right there!" Christina looked up to see three police officers racing toward them. Elvis quickly explained what was happening and the police arrested Manendra and the man in the gray suit.

"Thank you, Mimi!" Christina said. "You made sure the police got here just in time!"

Soman and Shiba purred like kittens as the twins hugged them like teddy bears. Lifting her tear-stained face from Shiba's fur, Asha exclaimed, "There's still time!"

"Time for what?" Christina asked.

"The show!" Asha replied.

With all the commotion, Christina had forgotten all about the show. Spotting Mimi and Papa, who had just arrived, she ran to them in a panic.

"Have you ever chauffeured tigers, Papa?" she asked.

"There's a first time for everything!" he replied.

Christina and Grant couldn't help giggling at the white tigers sitting in the back seat of the yellow Hummer with Asha and Chandu. The twins grinned and waved as Papa, now a tiger chauffeur, pulled away from the curb.

Families packed the Mysteries Hotel theater to see the magic show. Christina was relieved to see Chandu and Asha brilliantly fill the magician's role. Despite their ordeal, the tigers also performed perfectly. And this time, when Soman and Shiba disappeared, they also reappeared!

20 WHAT HAPPENS IN VEGAS...

"The show's a hit!" a jovial Mr. Jenkins said the next morning at breakfast. "Thanks to all of you, I can save the hotel and help with tiger rescue efforts.

"And now," Mr. Jenkins continued, "I'd like you to meet my new magician—Elvis!"

"Thank you, thank you very much!" Elvis said, as he made a grand entrance to the breakfast table.

"That's great news," Christina said to Elvis. "But I need some answers. For a while, I thought you were the bad guy."

"Sorry about that, Christina," Elvis said. "I was installing a sign at a new resort when I overheard the owner and Manendra talking about stealing the tigers from the Mysteries Hotel. The owner offered me a job if I'd keep my mouth shut and help them."

"Why didn't you tell the police?" Grant asked.

"Because the owner threatened to harm the tigers if I told the police," Elvis explained. "I wanted to stick around and keep an eye on them. When I rescued you kids in the desert, I realized you were smart and could figure out my clues."

"I guess this means you're going home," Christina said sadly to Chandu and Asha.

"No, we get to stay!" Asha cried. "Papa is going to teach Elvis to be a tiger trainer."

"That's right," Chandu said. "Our parents have made arrangements for someone to take care of the rescue tigers in India for a while and our mother is coming to join us here."

"We're even signing up for school," Asha added.

"WHAT?" Grant shouted. "You had it made! Why did you sign up for school?"

"Hey, Grant," Christina said, "there are some people who actually like to go to school! Besides, it's the law!"

"I don't dislike school," Grant said, "I'd just like to see more recess and longer lunches!"

"OK, kids," Papa said to Christina and Grant. "The *Mystery Girl* is waiting! We need to get going."

As they all said goodbye, Elvis suddenly sneezed loudly.

"AH-CHOOO!!"

"That's funny," Christina said. "I don't seem to have my cold anymore. I guess I gave it to you."

"Makes perfect sense," Elvis said. "You know what they say, *What happens in Vegas, stays in Vegas!*"

THE END

About the Author

Carole Marsh is an author and publisher who has written many works of fiction and non-fiction for young readers. She travels throughout the United States and around the world to research her books. In 1979 Carole Marsh was named Communicator of the Year for her corporate communications work with major national and international corporations.

Marsh is the founder and CEO of Gallopade International, established in 1979. Today, Gallopade International is widely recognized as a leading source of educational materials for every state and many countries. Marsh and Gallopade were recipients of the 2004 Teachers' Choice Award. Marsh has written more than 50 Carole Marsh Mysteries™. In 2007, she was named Georgia Author of the Year. Years ago, her children, Michele and Michael, were the original characters in her mystery books. Today, they continue the Carole Marsh Books tradition by working at Gallopade. By adding grandchildren Grant and Christina as new mystery characters, she has continued the tradition for a third generation.

Ms. Marsh welcomes correspondence from her readers. You can e-mail her at fanclub@gallopade.com, visit carolemarshmysteries.com, or write to her in care of Gallopade International, P.O. Box 2779, Peachtree City, Georgia, 30269 USA.

Built-In Book Club

Talk About It!

1. Asha and Chandu loved their white tigers. Some people keep tigers as pets, although they are truly wild animals and can be dangerous. Do you think you would like to have a tiger as a pet?

2. Grant and Christina used many different forms of transportation in the book, including an airplane, a Hummer, a monorail, a gondola, and a trolley. Of all the forms of transportation you have used, which is your favorite?

3. One of Jack's jobs was working as an Elvis impersonator. If you could impersonate a famous person, who would it be?

4. Have you visited Las Vegas? If so, what was your favorite activity? If not, what was your favorite activity that Grant and Christina did in the book?

5. Grant and Christina rode some pretty scary roller coasters in Las Vegas. Have you ever been on a roller coaster? If so, how did it make you feel? Where is your favorite roller coaster?

6. The kids visited the Ethel M. Chocolate factory in Las Vegas. Have you ever been to a factory where food was made? If so, what type of food was made there?

7. Grant and Christina went to the Las Vegas Natural History Museum. Do you like to study history? If so, why? If not, why not?

8. Grant encountered a Gila monster while visiting Ice Box Canyon. Have you ever encountered a poisonous or dangerous animal? If so, describe your experience.

9. Grant, Christina, Asha, and Chandu found the tigers at the Flamingo being crowned King and Queen of the strip. Why do you think Manendra and the others did this?

10. Which character did you like the most? Which character was most like you?

Built-In Book Club

Bring it to Life!

1. Use the Internet to research fun places in Las Vegas! Choose a book club member and plan a pretend trip to Las Vegas. Find the "perfect" hotel, choose the car that your family will rent, and choose at least three activities in Las Vegas! Make it fun—it's your vacation!

2. Pick a famous celebrity, historical figure, or sports figure. Use books or the Internet to learn interesting things about that person's life. Dress up and "impersonate" your choice at a book club meeting.

3. Grant and Christina had to figure out clues by looking at missing words or letters. Write

familiar phrases and leave out one of the words. Ask book club members to figure out the missing word. Here's an example: "Twinkle, twinkle, little _____."

4. Create a roller coaster! Divide into groups and gather art supplies like poster board, pencils, markers, crayons, and glitter. Design a roller coaster on your poster board. (If you really want to work hard, you could make a three-dimensional roller coaster out of popsicle sticks!) Make it fun! Make it flashy! Name it something fancy!

Glossary

chauffeur: a person employed to drive a car or limousine that transports passengers

concierge: a member of a hotel staff in charge of special services for guests, such as arranging for theater tickets or tours

damsel: a young woman or girl; a maiden, originally one of gentle or noble birth

dismay: discouragement; loss of courage in face of danger or disappointment

dumbfounded: shocked and speechless

elaborate: (adj.) rich in detail; fancy

feline: relating to animals of the cat family

impersonate: to act or play the part of a certain person or character

mesmerize: to hypnotize, captivate, or fascinate

observe: to see, watch, perceive, or notice

phantom: an appearance or illusion that is not real, such as a dream image, mirage, or optical illusion

scrutinize: to examine in detail with careful or critical attention

Las Vegas Trivia

1. There are about 125,000 hotel rooms in Las Vegas.

2. Vegas Vic, the enormous neon cowboy that towers over Fremont Street, is the world's largest mechanical neon sign.

3. More than 39 million people visit Las Vegas each year!

4. The Stratosphere is the tallest, free-standing, observation tower in the U.S. and the tallest structure west of the Mississippi River.

5. If you wanted to spend one night in every hotel room in Las Vegas, it would take you 288 years!

6. Construction workers at Hoover Dam had a mascot dog! You can visit the dog's grave near the Hoover Dam Tour Center.

7. There are about 15,000 miles of neon tubing on the Strip and in downtown Las Vegas!

8. The kangaroo rat, a resident of the Mojave Desert, can survive without drinking a drop of water—ever! They get liquid from plant seeds.

9. More gold is mined in Nevada than in any other state! Other gold-producing states include Alaska, California, Colorado, New Mexico, and Utah.

10. Every day, about 15,000 pillowcases are washed at the MGM Grand Hotel! (How would you like to fold them every day?)

Scavenger Hunt

Want to have some fun? Let's go on a scavenger hunt! See if you can find the items below related to the mystery. (*Teachers: You have permission to reproduce this page for your students.*)

1.____ A picture of Elvis

2.____ A piece of chocolate

3.____ A magic wand

4.____ Sunglasses

5.____ A picture of a white tiger

6.____ A map of Nevada

7.____ A cactus

8.____ A picture of Hoover Dam

9.____ Glitter

10.____ A digital camera

Pop Quiz

1. Where did the kids find Soman and Shiba in the end of the mystery?

2. Who picked up the kids, Mimi, and Papa when the *Mystery Girl* broke down in the desert?

3. What country did Asha and Chandu come from?

4. True or False? There are more orange tigers than white tigers.

5. What is the name of the hotel where Grant and Christina stayed?

6. Hoover Dam straddles two time zones. What are those time zones?

7. Where did the kids find Mr. Patel?

8. What are the statues made of in Madame Tussauds Museum?

WRITE YOUR OWN MYSTERY!

Make up a dramatic title!

You can pick four real kid characters!

Select a real place for the story's setting!

Try writing your first draft!

Edit your first draft!

Read your final draft aloud!

You can add art, photos or illustrations!